Date: 6/28/13

AVAILABLE NOW
from Lerner Publishing Services!

The *On the Hardwood* series:

Chicago Bulls
Dallas Mavericks
Los Angeles Clippers
Los Angeles Lakers
Miami HEAT
Minnesota Timberwolves
Oklahoma City Thunder
San Antonio Spurs

COMING SOON!

Additional titles in
the *On the Hardwood* series:

Boston Celtics
Brooklyn Nets
Houston Rockets
Indiana Pacers
New York Knicks
Philadelphia 76ers
Portland Trail Blazers
Utah Jazz

To Order   •   www.lernerbooks.com   •   800-328-4929   •   fax 800-332-1132

ON THE HARDWOOD

PETE BIRLE

On the Hardwood: Minnesota Timberwolves

MVP Books
2255 Calle Clara
La Jolla, CA 92037

MVP Books is an imprint of Book Buddy Digital Media, Inc., 42982 Osgood Road, Fremont, CA 94539

MVP Books publications may be purchased for
educational, business, or sales promotional use.

Cover and layout design by Jana Ramsay
Copyedited by Susan Sylvia
Photos by Getty Images

ISBN: 978-1-61570-507-8 (Library Binding)
ISBN: 978-1-61570-506-1 (Soft Cover)

TABLE OF CONTENTS

Chapter 1	An Unfortunate Injury	6
Chapter 2	Cold... But Not Lonely	14
Chapter 3	So Close	24
Chapter 4	Now What?	36
Chapter 5	Future Champs?	42

Midway through the lockout-shortened 2012 season, a poll on NBA.com asked users which professional basketball team was the biggest surprise of the year.

Fans answered clearly: The Minnesota Timberwolves were the top choice. The team had rebounded from just 32 victories over the previous two 82-game seasons to creep into the playoff picture in the Western Conference.

And then, on March 9, everything fell apart.

At home in the Target Center, the Timberwolves were giving the mighty Los Angeles Lakers a taste of how things had changed for the franchise

A Season Lost

The Timberwolves were headed for the playoffs when disaster struck in the form of a season-ending knee injury to rookie sensation Ricky Rubio.

from Minnesota. The Wolves were ahead 102-101, with less than 20 seconds to play. The Lakers had the ball and everyone in the building knew what was next.

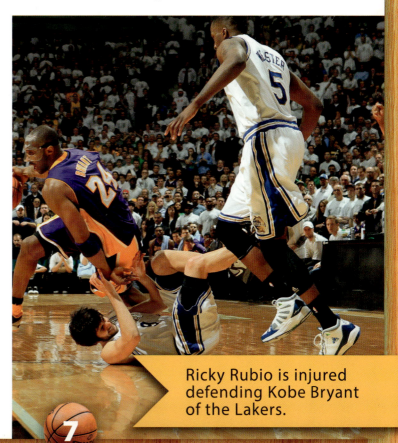

Ricky Rubio is injured defending Kobe Bryant of the Lakers.

All-Around Talent

Rubio was averaging 10.6 points and 8.2 assists per game, as well as leading the NBA in steals, when he tore his ACL.

Rubio looks to pass around Brandon Wright of the Mavericks.

The play would run through one of the league's best players and most dangerous offensive threats, Kobe Bryant.

Lakers center Pau Gasol held the ball at the top of the key, looking for Kobe on the left wing. He passed him the ball with 18 seconds on the clock. Immediately, Minnesota rookie guard Ricky Rubio left his man, Derek Fisher, to double-team Kobe along the sideline. Hoping to draw the charge with 16.4 seconds left in the game, Rubio was called for a block, as Bryant made contact with him. While the play didn't look like anything out of the ordinary, it was. Rubio suffered a freak injury when his and Kobe's knees bumped. It was the worst news both he and the Wolves could have heard. Rubio

Kevin Love, going to the basket against the Denver Nuggets, enjoyed a career year in 2011-12.

had torn his anterior cruciate (the dreaded ACL) and lateral collateral (LCL) ligaments in his left knee.

The 21-year-old from Spain underwent reconstructive surgery two weeks later in Vail, Colorado. His promising NBA debut season had been cut short. At the time of his injury, he was averaging 10.6 points and 8.2 assists per game—and leading the NBA in steals. He said in his first press conference after the surgery that he was hopeful that he would recover in time to take part in training camp—or even the start of the 2012-13 season.

Remaining Positive

Despite the uncertainty surrounding his being able to return for the start of the 2012-13 season, Rubio remained optimistic.

Rubio had played professionally in Spain for six seasons. Due to this experience, he remained optimistic. He displayed the upbeat attitude that Minnesota fans had come to love—along with his mad skills on the basketball court.

His teammate, All-Star power forward Kevin Love, also ended the 2012 season on the injured list. Love had been knocked dizzy in a game at Denver on April 11.

Although Love passed all the concussion tests and was cleared by the NBA to return to the court, Minnesota Coach Rick Adelman decided against playing Love. The combination of missed time and the sensitive nature of head injuries made a return unworthy of the risk. In other words, the Wolves didn't want to take any chances with the other face of their franchise.

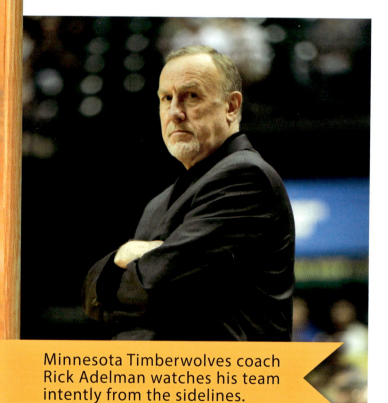

Minnesota Timberwolves coach Rick Adelman watches his team intently from the sidelines.

Love was fourth in the league with 26 points per game, and second in rebounding with 13.3 per game when he was knocked down and out.

The Wolves experienced a dramatic fall in the Western Conference standings. Minnesota compiled a forgettable 5-20 record after Rubio went down to end the season at 26-40—and out of the playoffs.

But things are definitely looking up for Minnesota. Under the guidance of veteran NBA coach Adelman, Love and Rubio woke up the Wolves. The duo injected life into a club—and fan base—that's been stuck in a draft-pick nightmare for the last seven years. They've desired a one-two

Rubio and Love injected life into a club and fan base hungry for a winner.

punch like Rubio and Love for just as long.

Rubio, had he not gone down with an injury, may have given Kyrie Irving a run for 2012 NBA Rookie of the Year. Even though the Wolves had to wait two years for his eventual arrival, Rubio was worth the wait—and better than advertised.

At 6'3", he's not big, but he plays big, and he makes big plays. Always scanning the defense, looking for the slightest weakness to exploit, he is today's version of "Pistol" Pete Maravich. Maravich was the 1970s

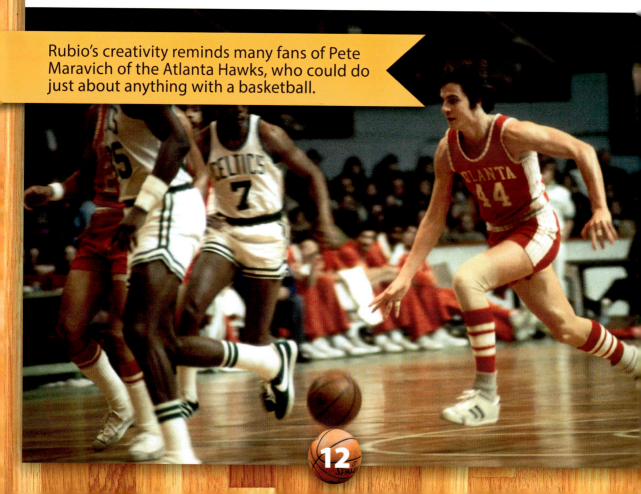

Rubio's creativity reminds many fans of Pete Maravich of the Atlanta Hawks, who could do just about anything with a basketball.

NBA star who could do just about anything he wanted to with a basketball in his hands. Due to the comparison, Rubio's nickname is "La Pistola"—the Pistol in Spanish.

Fond of no-look passes that often go between the legs of a defender, Rubio is equally as effective on the defensive end of the court. When watching him, don't look down, or away. Keep your eyes on him—because you never know what he's going to do.

As one Eastern Conference executive said, "He brings people out of their chairs, and he'll put them in your stands."

That much is true. But he—along

Rubio, guarded by Deron Williams of the Nets, attempts to hit a teammate with a creative pass.

with Love—just might also bring Minnesota that NBA championship the franchise and city crave so badly. Unfortunately, Wolves fans are just going to have to wait a little longer. ...

"La Pistola"
Rubio has been compared to the late NBA legend "Pistol" Pete Maravich. As a result, he is called "La Pistola," the Pistol in Spanish.

The state of Minnesota is called "The Land of 10,000 Lakes" because of all the bodies of water there. That's why the Lakers are who they are, even if Los Angeles isn't known for its ice fishing.

The Lakers played in Minneapolis from 1948 to 1960 until leaving for the West Coast. In the late '60s, Minneapolis was home to two teams in the old American Basketball Association (ABA), which merged with the NBA in the 1970s. But the city was left without basketball for two decades, until the Wolves arrived in 1989.

As it goes with most expansion teams, wins were hard to come by in the early

going. The team went 22-60 in its inaugural season. But the city was hungry for pro basketball. Playing in the enormous Metrodome, the Timberwolves drew over 1 million

The Wolves drew a record 1 million fans to the massive Metrodome in their inaugural season.

fans (an NBA record for attendance) for the 41 home games in their first year.

Those same fans had submitted more than 1,200 ideas for a contest to name the team. Choices were narrowed down to the Timberwolves and the Polars. The team put it to a vote among all the city councils in Minnesota, and it made sense that the Wolves won. There are more Timberwolves in Minnesota than in any state other than Alaska.

So, even though the basketball left much to be desired, the city loved its new team and new name. In year two, the Wolves moved up a spot, to fifth in the Midwest Division, with a 29-53 record. But year three ended the forward progression. An opening day blizzard that dumped 24 inches of snow was

Even when the basketball left much to be desired, the fans in Minneapolis loved their team and its Minnesota-inspired name.

a bad sign for the season. Minnesota lost that game, and nine of their first ten, on the way to a last-place finish in the NBA at 15-67. To make matters worse, in the off-season, the Wolves lost out on the chance to select Shaquille O'Neal by not getting the top pick in the Draft Lottery.

With no Shaq, the team looked to another college star instead: forward Christian Laettner, who had just led Duke to two consecutive national championships. Although Laettner had a solid rookie campaign, averaging 18.2 points and 8.7 rebounds per game, the Wolves finished 19-63.

Christian Laettner, a college star, joined the Wolves in 1992.

One of the few highlights during these early years—especially in the middle of a poor 20-62 season—

No Shaq Attack
The Wolves lost out on the chance to draft Shaquille O'Neal, so they selected Christian Laettner, who had just led Duke to consecutive NCAA Championships.

Isaiah Rider won the 1994 NBA Slam Dunk contest with his famous "East Bay Funk Dunk."

was when rookie Isaiah Rider made what Minnesota announcer Tom Hanneman called the "play of the decade."

With the ball going out of bounds on the left sideline, Rider flung the ball over his left shoulder, high in the air, with his back to the basket. It hit nothing but net for a three-pointer. He won an ESPY Award for the best NBA play of the year.

Rider brought the Wolves' faithful another memory when Minnesota's new arena, the Target Center, served as host of the 1994

All-Star Game. The fans went crazy when Isaiah Rider won the Slam Dunk Contest. The winning dunk was Rider's between-the-leg "East Bay Funk Dunk." Hailing from Oakland, California, in an area known as the East Bay, Rider dribbled down the baseline. Once there, he rose into the air, passed the ball between his legs and jammed it home as he flew past the rim.

It's still regarded as one of the greatest slams in All-Star Weekend history. Charles Barkley, who was commenting at courtside, said, "That may be the best dunk I've ever seen."

Despite its rabid fans, who supported the Wolves no matter their record, owners Marv Wolfenson and Harvey Ratner put the team up for sale. A group from Louisiana tried to buy the club and move the franchise to New Orleans. The NBA wanted the Wolves to stay in Minnesota, partly because the fans were so loyal. Glen Taylor bought the team and kept it in Minneapolis.

The next season was equally as forgettable, as the team went 21-61 to become the first NBA team to lose 60 or more games four years in a row. At the end of the season, former Boston Celtics star Kevin McHale, who played his college ball down the road at the University of Minnesota, took over as the

Funky Dunk
Charles Barkley said Isaiah Rider's "East Bay Funk Dunk" was possibly the best slam he'd ever seen.

Timberwolves' Vice President of basketball operations.

McHale quickly made two moves that had a lasting impact on the franchise. First, he made a bold selection in the 1995 NBA Draft, selecting high school phenom Kevin Garnett with the fifth overall pick.

Garnett was a gamble in the 1995 NBA Draft. But his potential— he stood close to seven feet and had a guard's feel for the game— was hard to overlook. McHale, a three-time NBA Champion with the Celtics, was among those fascinated by the kid. After six straight sub-.500 seasons since coming into the league, he felt the Wolves needed to take some chances.

Garnett's rookie season was a learning experience that began in training camp. Twice-a-day prac-tices under Coach Bill Blair were more strenuous than anything he had ever experienced. According to McHale's plan, Blair wasn't going to rush Garnett along. He used him off the bench to give forwards Tom Gugliotta and Laettner a rest.

But the first half of Garnett's rookie campaign was not what

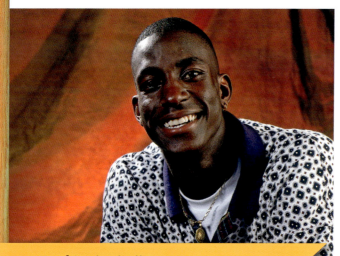

VP of Basketball Operations Kevin McHale made a bold selection with high school phenom Kevin Garnett.

McHale had hoped. With the team performing far under expectations, he replaced Blair with his old college roommate, Phil "Flip" Saunders. Two-time Coach of the Year in the Continental Basketball Association, Saunders injected new life into the Wolves. In Laettner's mind, though, Saunders directed too much attention toward Garnett. When the former Duke star told the media how he felt, McHale sent him packing.

Laettner's departure created an opportunity for Garnett. By the end of the year, he was averaging 10.4 points and 6.3 rebounds per game, good enough for the NBA All-Rookie Second Team. Though

Garnett grabs a rebound. He showed early signs of becoming an NBA star.

the Wolves finished 26-56, the year was considered a success. It was their second-best record yet, and Garnett was already showing signs of becoming an NBA superstar.

The 1992 "Dream Team"
Laettner was the lone college player on the 1992 U.S. Olympic Team, and was surrounded by 11 future NBA Hall of Famers.

Second, McHale went out and got someone to team up with KG (those are Garnett's initials and his nickname). He swapped Ray Allen to the Bucks for the rights to the fourth overall pick in 1996, point guard Stephon Marbury. Marbury had just completed his freshman year at Georgia Tech. He had an explosive first step to the basket and great range from the outside.

Garnett, Gugliotta and Marbury comprised three of the NBA's youngest stars. In 1996-97, they led the Wolves to a 40-42 record and the team's first-ever trip to the NBA playoffs. While Garnett was the youngest All-Star since Magic

Tom Gugliotta defends the Heat's Alonzo Mourning. In 1996-97, Gugliotta, Garnett and Stephon Marbury were three of the NBA's youngest and most exciting stars.

Johnson, it was the chemistry between Marbury and KG that made headlines. Their inside-outside game was poetry in motion. As Minnesota prepared for its opening-round playoff game against the Houston Rockets, fans hoped the young pair could help the Wolves pull off an upset. It wasn't to be, as the Rockets swept them in three. But the trip to the post-season would become a regular occurrence for the Wolves.

Unfortunately, despite making the playoffs eight consecutive times from 1997-2004, the Wolves lost in the first round in their first seven trips.

It wasn't until 2003-04 that Minnesota won its first division title and advanced past the first round of

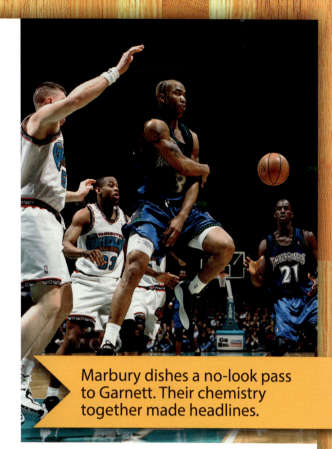

Marbury dishes a no-look pass to Garnett. Their chemistry together made headlines.

the playoffs.

And the fans who had loved their Wolves from the beginning were with them every step of the way.

Close, but No Cigar
Despite making the playoffs for eight years (1997-2004), the Wolves were ousted in the first round in their first seven trips to the post-season.

Chapter 3
SO CLOSE

The Wolves lost 60 games in each of the four seasons before Garnett arrived. In his second season, he helped lead them to the first of eight consecutive playoff appearances.

Unfortunately, as things were looking up on the hardwood, there was trouble off the court.

First, the club was punished by the NBA for making a secret deal with free agent forward Joe Smith to get around the league's salary cap rules. Before the 1998-99 season, Smith agreed in secret to sign three one-year contracts with the Timberwolves for less than what he could earn on the market. In return, he received a promise that the Timberwolves would give him a multi-year, multi-million dollar contract before the 2001-02 season.

Difference Maker

In each of the four seasons before Kevin Garnett arrived in Minnesota, the Wolves lost 60 games. But once he arrived, the fortunes of the franchise turned around.

After word of that secret agreement got out, the NBA Commissioner, David Stern, voided Smith's final one-year contract with

Joe Smith made a secret deal with the club to get around the league's salary rules.

McHale offered Garnett a contract that was worth more than the value of the entire franchise!

McHale for an entire season. The penalty was one of the stiffest in league history and proved devastating to the Wolves.

That single penalty crippled Minnesota's chances at giving Garnett a championship-quality supporting cast. They had no first-round picks for several years, missing out on such players as Kenyon Martin, Zach Randolph, Pau Gasol, Joe Johnson, Yao Ming, Tony Parker, and Dwight Howard. What a difference even one of those players might have made!

Then, there was the issue of Garnett's contract. After holding out for a better deal, Garnett finally got

the Timberwolves, making him a free agent. Stern also took away three of the Timberwolves' next five first-round draft picks (two were ultimately returned), fined the team $3.5 million and suspended

McHale to give in, signing KG to a six-year, $126 million contract. This deal was for $18 million more than the team's original offer. It was more money than the estimated value of the Timberwolves. This was the first time an athlete in a major sport was owed more money than the suggested worth of the entire franchise.

Criticized by the media for being greedy and selfish, Garnett was now expected to win. After an up-and-down start, the Wolves won 14 of 16. Gugliotta was quietly becoming one of the best in the game, along with Garnett and Marbury, and the team was getting solid contributions from

reserve centers Stanley Roberts and Cherokee Parks. In January, KG led the Timberwolves to a franchise-record seven wins in a row. He

Garnett was the main reason for the team's winning campaigns in the late 1990s and early 2000s.

27

notched his first career triple-double against the Denver Nuggets, scoring 18 points, grabbing 13 rebounds and dishing out 10 assists. He also became the first player in franchise history to start in the All-Star Game.

Minnesota ended the season at 45-37. At 18 points, 9.6 rebounds and 4.2 assists per game, Garnett was the primary reason for the team's first winning campaign. He broke the team's single-season records for rebounds, double-doubles (points and rebounds each over 10) and minutes played.

But after winning two of the first three games in their opening playoff series vs. the Seattle SuperSonics, the Wolves collapsed. Seattle guard Gary Payton got hot, and the Sonics took the five-game series.

To make matters worse, a lockout by NBA owners—triggered in part by Garnett's contract—suspended the start of the 1998-99 season. When the dust settled, Gugliotta was gone. Marbury was traded as well. He had become increasingly unhappy playing in the shadow of Garnett's contract.

Lastly, there was the death of Malik Sealy in May 2000, the Wolves' talented and popular small forward. Sealy had been promoted to the starting lineup the season before. Then he was gone. Sealy was killed by a drunk driver on his way home

Aftershocks

Triggered partly by Garnett's contract, the NBA owners suspended the start of the 1998-99 season. Soon after, both Gugliotta and Marbury were gone from the Wolves.

from a birthday celebration for Garnett, his best friend.

Garnett took his friend's death especially hard. But the 2003 All-Star Game in Atlanta helped ease his pain. It was supposed to be Michael Jordan's "farewell" to the league and his fans, but KG made the game his own. In a close and exciting contest that went into overtime, Jordan made a shot to give the East a one-point lead with less than five seconds

Malik Sealy, the Wolves' talented and popular small forward, dishes to a teammate against the Trail Blazers.

Garnett's Time to Shine

Garnett upstaged Michael Jordan in Jordan's final All-Star Game by scoring 37 points, and grabbing nine rebounds. He ran away with the All-Star Game's MVP award.

to go. Kobe Bryant then tied the score for the West with a free throw, sending the game into double OT.

From that point, it was all Garnett, who was playing guard for Coach Phil Jackson, despite being 6'11". Three times, he hit short jumpers over Vince Carter. The West held on to win by 10, 155-145, but the spotlight was reserved for Garnett, who finished with 37 points, nine rebounds and five steals. The last player to score that many points in an All-Star Game was Jordan, with 40 in 1988. Despite Jordan being the sentimental favorite, Garnett ran away with the game's MVP award.

Back at home, an interesting trend seemed to be developing. The Wolves seemed to play their best when Garnett was not their top scorer. They were more successful when he did more of the little things. He passed up scoring opportunities to involve his teammates more, especially second-year forward Wally Szczerbiak and newcomer, guard Chauncey Billups.

But another quick exit in the playoffs, after posting a franchise-best 51-31 regular season record, left fans wondering if Garnett could bring Minnesota a championship. He had established himself as one of the league's top players, and he finished second to the Spurs' Tim Duncan in the voting for NBA MVP. But seven straight first-round losses was becoming a bit frustrating for the team and the fan base.

In 2003-04, McHale again set about trying to find the right supporting cast for Garnett. His two biggest acquisitions were point guard Sam Cassell and swingman Latrell Sprewell. Cassell was a proven winner; he worked the pick and roll with Garnett to perfection. And Sprewell played hard every minute of every game. The result was 58 wins and the best record in the West.

Garnett was hands down the best player in the NBA. Averaging 24.2 points, a league-high 13.9 rebounds, and 5.0 assists, he joined Larry Bird as the only players to average at least 20 points, 10 rebounds and 5.0 assists for five consecutive years. He won the MVP in a landslide, taking 120 of 123 votes. He also became the first

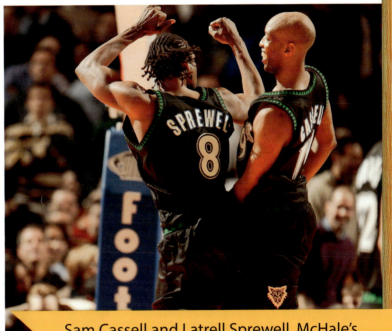

Sam Cassell and Latrell Sprewell, McHale's two biggest acquisitions in 2003-04, celebrate a victory against the Knicks.

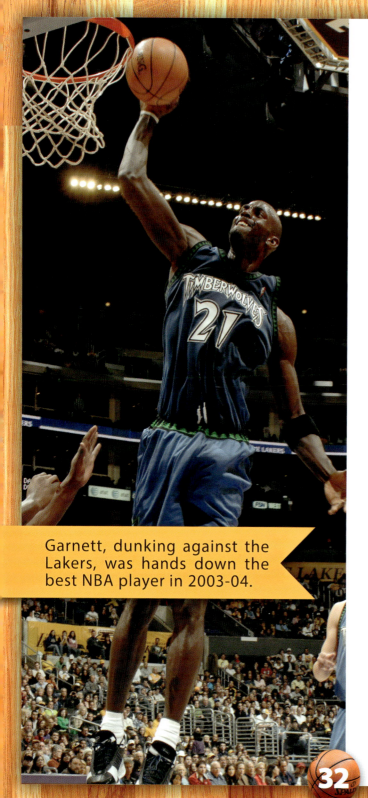

Garnett, dunking against the Lakers, was hands down the best NBA player in 2003-04.

player in 29 years to lead the league in total points scored and rebounds.

Up first for Minnesota in the playoffs was Denver with their lights-out rookie Carmelo Anthony. The Wolves disposed of Denver easily. Cassell hit for 40 in Game 1, while Garnett averaged just under 30 points a night in the five-game series.

Advancing to the second round was a relief for KG, who had never been able to take the team there. After losing the first game to the Kings, 104-98, and despite another 40 points from Cassell, the Wolves looked to avoid going down 0-2 at home. Behind by 10 with four minutes to go in Game 2, the Wolves went on a 16-1 run to beat the Kings, 94-89. Then, in Game 3, Garnett scored 30 points and grabbed 15 boards in a thrilling 114-113 overtime win. KG also nailed the game-winning shot. But the Kings won two of the next three to force Game 7 in the Target Center.

In the most pressure-packed game of his life, and the biggest game in Timberwolves history, Garnett showed what he was made of. Coming back from taking an elbow to the face in Game 6, he scored 32 points, snagged 21 rebounds, blocked five shots and had four steals. He was on the floor for an amazing 46 of 48 minutes!

With six minutes remaining in the game, the noise in the Target Center was deafening. The Minnesota fans were banging

inflatable noise-makers (called "thunder sticks") and screaming for their Wolves to stay strong down the stretch. Feeding off the passion and energy of the crowd, the Wolves seemed to respond. Every time

In the most pressure-packed game of his life, Garnett came up big, time and again.

33

Garnett seems to come out of nowhere to swat Brad Miller's shot with only seconds left in the game.

Garnett touched the ball, the crowd yelled louder, and he came through. It was like they gave him a shot of energy that he, in turn, handed out to his teammates.

At one point in the fourth quarter, he scored 10 points in a row. With five minutes left in the game and the Wolves up 72-68, Garnett put a crossover move on Chris Webber that left him in the dust and he threw down a monster jam. Garnett was doing exactly what an MVP should do: Put the team on his shoulders and carry them to victory.

The Wolves led 83-80 with four seconds left in the game when the Kings' Mike Bibby found Doug Christie on the right wing. Christie launched a long three-pointer for Sacramento. The shot missed everything. But the Kings' Brad Miller caught the air ball and looked like he was set for an easy layup. Instead, Garnett seemed to come from out of nowhere to swat Miller's shot into the seats with just a few ticks left on the clock. On the inbounds play, Sacramento passed the ball cross-court to Webber, but his shot went in and out.

Garnett leaped onto the scorer's table and soaked up the cheers of the crowd—on his 28th birthday.

Next up were the Los Angeles Lakers in the Western Conference Finals. Picked to win it all from before the season started, the Lakers' lineup of four future Hall of Famers—Kobe, Shaq, Gary Payton, and Karl Malone—were just too

Broad Shoulders

In Game 7, Garnett did what MVPs are supposed to do: He put his team on his shoulders and carried the Wolves to victory.

tough (and too playoff-tested) for the Wolves.

Minnesota came close, but lost to L.A. in six. After Cassell went down with an injury, the Wolves, despite Garnett's efforts, couldn't pull off the upset.

Garnett revels in the crowd's cheers after the Wolves won Game 7 against the Kings—on his 28th birthday.

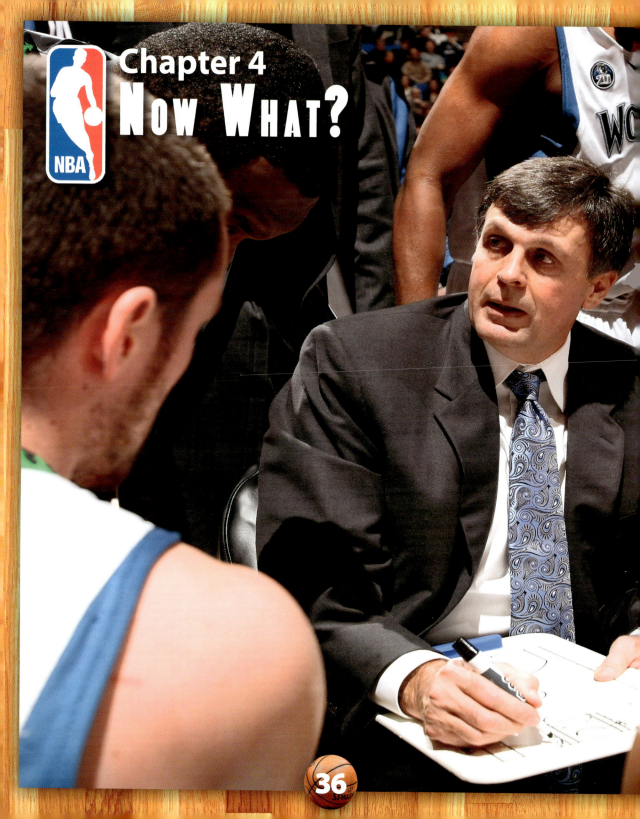

With Minnesota's exciting play-off push—ultimately coming within two wins of the NBA Finals—behind them, it seemed like 2004-05 would right the wrong.

But it wasn't to be. There were problems from the start, as Cassell and Sprewell indicated how unhappy they were with their contracts. With the Wolves playing unevenly most of the season, McHale tried to shake things up by firing Saunders and inserting himself as coach. That didn't work and set the stage for three years of underachievement. In 2006-07, they could only muster 32 wins. Their appearance in the Western Conference Finals seemed like a distant memory.

Minnesota had replaced two coaches and not made the playoffs since that exciting run in '04. McHale once again had to do something. The club needed a change. A big one.

Garnett, who didn't have much talent around him at this point in time, never said he was unhappy and never asked to be traded. But he quietly asked management to upgrade the Timberwolves' roster. Among only five players in NBA history with at least 19,000 points, 10,000 rebounds and 4,000 assists, Garnett had been Minnesota's best player for more than 10 years. And he wanted to play for a true contender.

"It was time we had to make

Part of the Learning Curve
After McHale inserted himself as head coach, the Timberwolves experienced three up-and-down seasons under his leadership.

Garnett was traded to the Celtics in 2007 in the NBA's biggest trade ever for one player.

On July 31, 2007, Garnett was traded to the Boston Celtics for young stars Al Jefferson and Ryan Gomes, Theo Ratfliff, Gerald Green, Sebastian Telfair, two first-round draft picks and cash. Besides Ratliffe, who was 34 at the time, the other four were 24 years old or younger. The seven-for-one deal was the NBA's biggest trade for one player.

a decision on the direction of this team, look toward the future and try to figure out the best way we can develop a team that has a better record and better success than we've had," said Taylor, the Wolves' owner.

"The past few seasons our on-court performance has been disappointing to our fans, myself, [owner] Glen Taylor and the entire organization," said McHale. "Through this trade, we have obtained very talented, young players with a lot of potential, future flexibility with the salary cap and two future first-round NBA Draft picks."

Al Jefferson was the key player in the trade, and he played well his first season in Minnesota. But he couldn't fill the shoes left by KG's departure. The Wolves could only put together 22 wins in 2007-08. The next year, McHale left the front office again to coach the team, but the Wolves lost 13 straight games and sat at 4-23 on Christmas Day. Jefferson suffered a season-ending knee injury in early

Seven for One
The Wolves obtained four talented young players, one seasoned veteran and two future first-round draft picks in the Garnett trade.

Al Jefferson was the key piece in the Garnett trade, but he couldn't fill KG's shoes and was eventually dealt to Utah.

Love set a new franchise record with 31 points and 31 rebounds against the Knicks.

The Wolves went 15-67 in 2009-10, matching their worst mark in franchise history. Last season, they were still trying to find their identity in the wake of the Garnett trade. They seemed to find it during one week in November. Forward Michael Beasley, acquired in the off-season from the Heat, scored 42 against the Kings. Then, second-year forward/center Love scored 31 points and snagged 31 rebounds, setting a new franchise record, against the Knicks. It was the first 30-30 game in the NBA in 28 years.

In fact, Love—a UCLA graduate whose father Stan played with the

February, and the team finished 24-58. At the end of the year, McHale was dismissed.

Showing the Love

Kevin Love had a breakout season in 2010-11. He was named the league's Most Improved Player and was selected to the All-Star Team, the Wolves' first All-Star since Garnett.

Washington Bullets—had a break-out year for the Wolves in 2010-11. Named the league's Most Improved Player, he also was selected to the All-Star team, the Wolves' first All-Star since Garnett in 2007. On March 8, he broke the record of consecutive double-doubles. Eventually, his run ended at 53 on March 13, the longest such streak since 1976. He finished the season with 20.8 points per game and an NBA-best 15.2 rebounds per game, for the first 20-point and 15-rebound season average since Moses Malone in 1983. But despite Love's amazing campaign, the Wolves still had a rough season, finishing with an NBA-worst record of 17-65.

So management replaced Coach Kurt Rambis with Adelman. Love was suddenly the new face of the franchise. And they prepared for Rubio's arrival.

Coach Kurt Rambis was let go after the Wolves finished the year at 17-65, the worst record in the league.

Chapter 5
FUTURE CHAMPS?

Things were a bit different at the 2012 Rising Stars Challenge during All-Star Weekend in Orlando, Florida. This year's event had a different format, with the rookie and second-year players mixed together on teams for the first time. Former stars Shaquille O'Neal and Charles Barkley served as general managers who drafted their squads.

If you ever see any footage from that game, you'll see why Rubio is Spain's answer to Pete Maravich. With no real defensive effort and plenty of fan-pleasing fast breaks and flashy play, "La Pistola" was in his element. Playing for Shaq's squad, he turned routine passes to his teammates into behind-the-back and between-the-leg looks.

It was classic Rubio, and it's why the folks in Minnesota are so excited—and why his season-ending injury was so devastating.

Ricky Rubio works his magic, passing the ball behind his back, in the 2012 Rising Stars Challenge.

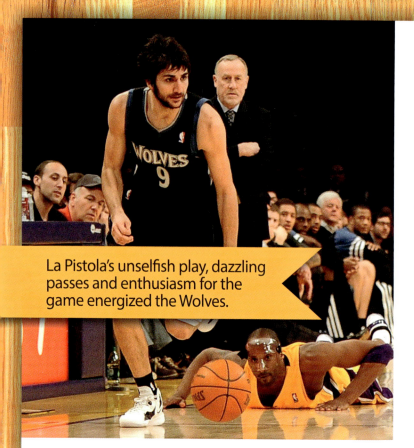

La Pistola's unselfish play, dazzling passes and enthusiasm for the game energized the Wolves.

The Timberwolves fully expected Rubio to return to the player who energized the franchise with unselfish play, dazzling passes and wild enthusiasm. The timeline for his return was less certain. Recovery time for an ACL injury is typically 9-12 months. However, one good thing was that the LCL (the other half of Rubio's injury) is considered to be the least important of the four major ligaments in the knee. Minnesota Vikings running back Adrian Peterson tore his in 2007 and only missed two games.

"You just have to be strong and do your best to try to come back even harder," said Rubio. "I love playing basketball, and I'm going to do my best to play again."

There's always a chance when Ricky Rubio brings the ball up the court that he's going to do

A Dangerous Asset

Rubio not only has great vision on the court, but he anticipates what is going to happen next, moves without the ball, and is a master thief on defense.

something magical. He acts as a coach on the floor. In the mold of Steve Nash, he has excellent vision. He anticipates well, moves without the ball and loves to deflect the ball on defense. He admits to practicing no-look passes, trying to be like Maravich, whom he has seen in videos.

Says Marc Calderon, his former U14 coach: "He reads basketball at a [speed] very few can achieve."

As the Wolves wrapped up another disappointing season, Adelman indicated how unhappy he was with the way his team responded to the injuries to Rubio and Love. He hinted that a major makeover was needed to add veterans to a young and immature squad.

The Wolves didn't respond well after stars Rubio and Love went down with injuries.

"It's going to be a really big summer," Adelman said. "I don't think we can be non-aggressive this summer. We have to strike and

Small forward Derrick Williams soars above the rim in a game against the Denver Nuggets.

(poor) April again," he added. "It's too hard. We have a better group than that."

The Wolves went on a shopping spree after the 2011-12 season. Minnesota signed veterans Brandon Roy, Andrei Kirilenko, and Greg Stiemsma. The team also took a flyer on Alexey Shved, a Russian shooting guard. Despite 13 players on the roster under age 30, a core of talent was there. Small forward Derrick Williams (the second pick in the 2011 draft, who made the NBA All-Rookie second team and averaged 8.8 points and 4.7 rebounds this

see who we can add to this group. I really believe if we come back healthy, that's a big thing, and you add a couple pieces, then we're in the mix because we were in the mix before all these injuries.

"I don't want to go through the

past season) is the real deal. And Nikola Pekovic (the Wolves 6'11" center from Europe, picked in the second round in 2008), is a solid post-up player who can wear opponents down.

"If I can do some magic, I do it," said Rubio. "But basketball isn't one-on-one. It's five-on-five, plus the bench."

Room to Grow

The Wolves have plenty of money to attract free agents and assist in making trades, which may help bring Minnesota the championship their loyal fans have been waiting for.

For the Minnesota Timberwolves and their loyal fans, they will need everyone healthy as they try to create magic with Rubio and climb the NBA's mountaintop.

Guard J.J. Barea pumps his fist on his way down the court, energized by the enthusiastic cheers of the Wolves' loyal fans.